S0-AZR-134

To Alexandra.
a spectacular firebird!
Happy Halloween '96!
Love, Sara, Joey,
Ben + Becca

BAREFOOT BOOKS

The barefoot child symbolizes the human being whose natural integrity and capacity for action are
unimpaired. In this spirit, Barefoot Books publishes new and traditional myths, legends, and fairy
tales whose themes demonstrate the pitfalls and dangers that surround our passage through life; the
qualities that are needed to face and overcome these dangers; and the equal importance of action and
reflection in doing so. Our intention is to present stories from a wide range of cultures in such a way
as to delight and inspire readers of all ages while honoring the tradition from which the story has
been inherited.

Prince Ivan and the Firebird

BAREFOOT BOOKS, INC.

the children's books imprint of Shambhala Publications, Inc.

Horticultural Hall

300 Massachusetts Avenue

Boston, Massachusetts 02115

This book has been printed on 100% acid-free paper

Text © 1994 by Cherry Gilchrist

Illustrations © 1994 by Andrei Troshkov

First published in Great Britain in 1994 by Barefoot Books Ltd

First published in the United States of America in 1994 by Barefoot Books, Inc.

All rights reserved. No part of this book may be reproduced in any form or by any means,

electronic or mechanical, including photocopying, recording, or by any information storage

and retrieval system, without permission in writing from the publisher.

Printed in Belgium by Proost International Book Production

9 8 7 6 5 4 3 2 1

Distributed in the United States by Random House, Inc.,

and in Canada by Random House of Canada, Ltd.

Library of Congress Cataloging-in-Publication-Data

Gilchrist, Cherry

Prince Ivan and the Firebird/retold by Cherry Gilchrist; illustrations by Andrei Troshkov.

p. cm.

Summary: When the youngest son of a King sets out to find the firebird which has been stealing golden apples from

his father's tree, he meets a gray wolf who helps him with his quest.

ISBN 1-56957-920-2 (acid-free paper)

[1. Fairy Tales. 2. Folklore – Russia.] I. Troshkov, Andrei, ill.II. Zhar-ptitsa. III. Title.

PZ8.G8Pr 1994

[398.21] – dc20

93-38136

CIP

AC

Prince Ivan and the Firebird

Retold by

CHERRY GILCHRIST

Illustrations by

ANDREI TROSHKOV

BAREFOOT BOOKS

BOSTON & BATH

Prince Ivan and the Firebird

There was once a king called Vyslav who had a very fine orchard, the best in the whole world. It was full of rare trees, but the king's favorite was one on which golden apples grew. Now one night a thief came into the orchard and began stealing these precious golden apples. But who could this thief be? Surely no person could creep past the guards and rob the orchard night after night. Every morning more of the fruit was missing, and every morning the king grew more and more angry. No one could solve the mystery.

King Vyslav had three sons, and he called them to help him. "My fine children, who can stop this happening? Whoever can catch the thief shall have half of my kingdom while I am alive, and the other half when I am dead." All three princes called out together that they would try to catch the thief.

The first chance was given to Prince Dmitri, the eldest. He went into the orchard that evening and sat down quietly under the golden-apple tree. What could be easier, he thought, than to grab hold of the robber and claim half the kingdom? But while he was enjoying these thoughts, he felt very sleepy, and soon drifted off into a deep slumber. And when he awoke, it was morning, and more of the golden apples were missing.

Prince Dmitri was too ashamed to tell his father what had happened.

"Did you catch the thief?" asked the king.

"Oh no, my Lord! I watched all night, and no one came near the tree."

But the king soon found that there were fewer apples on the tree than before, and so the next night he ordered his second son, Prince Vassily, into the orchard. Prince Vassily sat down under the tree as Dmitri had done, and prepared to guard it all night. But he too fell fast asleep, and woke to find the orchard robbed and the thief gone.

"Have you caught the thief?" his father asked the next morning. Prince Vassily, like his brother, was too proud to admit he had fallen asleep, and answered, "No, my gracious Lord, I kept watch but the thief did not appear. I think that someone is using magic; perhaps he has learned how to make himself invisible."

But King Vyslav did not believe this, and when he saw how many more of the golden apples were gone, he let out a furious roar. He turned to his youngest son, Prince Ivan, and said, "You are my only hope now. Do your best to save my golden apples. Soon there will be none left."

So that night Ivan too sat down beneath the apple tree, but, unlike his brothers, he stayed awake not just one hour, but two, and three. And then suddenly the whole orchard was ablaze with light, as if the sun had risen at midnight. It was the Firebird. The Firebird had come, with wings that shone like gold and eyes that gleamed like crystal. She perched in the tree, and began to pluck the apples with her beak of glowing amber. Prince Ivan tried to seize her. He moved as stealthily as he could, but the Firebird was quicker than him, and flew out of his grasp, leaving just one tail-feather behind in the prince's hand.

Early next morning Prince Ivan went to see his father, as his two elder brothers had done.

"Have you caught the thief?" asked King Vyslav.

"No, your Majesty," answered Ivan honestly. "But I know who it is. It is the Firebird. She has been stealing your golden apples." And he showed his father what he had snatched from her tail.

The feather was so glorious that the king immediately forgot about his orchard. It was full of brilliance, like a thousand candles all alight at once. The king put it in a room set aside for the most precious treasures of the kingdom. Now his only thought was to catch the Firebird herself. But though everyone waited, and watched, the Firebird did not come back to the orchard again.

Once more, King Vyslav sent for his three sons. "My dear children! Bring the Firebird back to me alive, and my kingdom is yours, as promised. Go now, and find this wondrous bird."

The two eldest princes received their father's blessing, and rode off together, jealous of Ivan for capturing the feather, and determined to do better than him this time. Ivan also asked for the king's blessing, but his father was not happy to let him go. "My dear son, you are too young for such a long and dangerous journey. What if you never return? I will have no sons at home, and it would break my heart if I were to die without any children. Who would rule the kingdom then? Stay here, and I will protect you."

But nothing he could say would persuade Prince Ivan to stay at home, and so, very reluctantly, the king gave him permission to leave.

Prince Ivan chose the finest horse in the royal stables, and set out. He did not know where he should go, but go he must, and so he rode bravely off into unknown lands.

After some time, he found himself on a great grassy plain, and in the middle of this plain was a stone pillar on which were carved the following words:

Straight ahead lies hunger and cold.
To the right – life and health to you, but death to your horse.
To the left – death to you, but life and health to your horse.

Ivan thought about this. If he took the right-hand path, at least he would still be alive, even if his horse was killed. He might be able to find another horse, but he could not replace his own life. And to go straight ahead promised no good to anyone. So he chose the right-hand path, and it wasn't long – three days at the most – before he saw a huge gray wolf walking toward him along the path. Fear almost made his heart stop beating.

"Hail, Prince Ivan, foolish boy. Did you not read the message on the stone? Did you not know that your horse would die if you came this way? So be it." And the wolf tore Ivan's horse limb from limb, devoured it, then ran away into the wilderness.

The prince was bitterly upset to see his horse dead, but he was determined not to give up his journey now. He walked and walked until he was so tired he thought he would drop, and then, suddenly Gray Wolf was there in front of him again. "Well," thought Ivan, "if I must die, I must die. So be it."

But Gray Wolf did not eat him up. Instead he said, "I am sorry, Prince Ivan, that I had to eat your horse. Now get up on my back, and I will carry you instead. Where are you going?"

"I am going to seek the Firebird."

"Ah well, you are in luck. I know just where she is. Jump on, and we will set off straight away."

Gray Wolf ran swifter than a horse, and soon after nightfall brought the prince to a fine palace, surrounded by a stone wall.

"Dismount, Ivan, and climb over the wall into the garden. There you will find the Firebird. But take care! She lives in a golden cage, and if you try to take the cage too, you will never come out alive. Do not forget my warning!"

So the prince climbed over the wall. Sure enough, the garden was filled with a wonderful light. The Firebird sat in her beautiful golden cage, preening her exquisite feathers. Ivan approached her cage, and was just about to lift her out of it, when he thought, "Oh, but it would be foolish to leave such a fine cage behind! And what will I carry the Firebird in, if I have no cage?" So he ignored the words of Gray Wolf, and took hold of the cage. But the cage was attached to all the trees in the garden by invisible wires, and all the trees were hung with bells, and no sooner had he touched it than the whole garden rang with a terrible jangling noise. Armed guards came running into the garden, and seized the prince, and dragged him like a common thief into the palace before their king himself.

"Who are you, you robber!" shouted the king in anger. "You have tried to steal my precious Firebird. You shall be put to death for this!"

Ivan replied, "I am Prince Ivan, the son of King Vyslav."

"Why did you not say this before?" said King Dolmat, for this was his name. "If you had asked me, I would have given the Firebird to you. Now I have no choice except to punish you as a thief, for you have broken the laws of our kingdom. However..." he paused, "there is perhaps one way out of this. If you can bring me the Horse with the Golden Mane that lives in the Thrice-Nine Land, I will give you the Firebird in exchange, and pardon you."

Ivan did not know where to find such a horse, but he agreed, and hastened away to where Gray Wolf was waiting for him.

"You did not listen to me," said Gray Wolf.

"I am sorry," replied the prince.

"So be it," said Gray Wolf. "Climb on to my back, and I will take you where you need to go."

Ivan climbed on to Gray Wolf's back, and away they went, faster than a horse, faster than an arrow shot from a bow.

At last, after nightfall, they came to the kingdom of the king who owned the Horse with the Golden Mane; King Afron was his name. Gray Wolf stopped in front of the royal stables, which were built of white stone, and told the prince to get down. "Go in there, Prince Ivan, and fetch the Horse with the Golden Mane while the guards are asleep. But remember! Take only the horse, and not the golden bridle that you will see hanging on the wall. If you touch it, you will never come out alive."

So Ivan climbed down, and crept into the stables after the guards were asleep. And there he saw the finest horse he had ever set eyes on, a beautiful white animal with a flowing golden mane and tail. But as he went to lead the horse out of the stable, he caught sight of a superb golden bridle, wrought with extraordinary craftmanship. He reached out to touch it – and all at once the stable was full of the most terrible din, for here were invisible strings attached to the bridle which set off the alarms all around him. The stable guards came running, and seized him. They dragged him into the palace, and threw him down roughly at the feet of King Afron.

Once again, Ivan was accused of being a common thief.

"Who are you, anyway?" demanded the king crossly when his rage had subsided.

"Your Majesty," answered Ivan, bowing low, "I am Prince Ivan, the youngest son of King Vyslav."

"Why did you not say so?" said the king grumpily. "You could have had the horse if you had come and asked me. Now there is nothing for you but shame and punishment, unless..." he hesitated, "you can bring me the lovely Princess Helen, who lives in the Thrice-Ten Kingdom. Oh, how I long for her! I love her with all my heart, but I have never yet been able to win her. If you can bring her to me, you shall have the Horse with the Golden Mane as a reward and walk away a free man."

What could Prince Ivan do but agree to this? When he left the palace, Gray Wolf was waiting. Once again, he shook his head sorrowfully when he heard what Ivan had done. "You forgot what I told you. Now we have an even more difficult task to accomplish. But I will help you. Jump on to my back, and we will go in search of Princess Helen the Fair."

So they sped away, faster than an arrow shot from a bow, until they came to the magnificent gardens, surrounded with golden railings, where Princess Helen was to be found.

"Jump down," said Gray Wolf. "This is a task that only I can accomplish. Walk back along the way we came, and wait for me on the open plain under the big green oak tree that we passed."

So Ivan left Gray Wolf, who waited all day by the golden railings, until the cool of the evening when Princess Helen came out with all her ladies-in-waiting to walk in the wonderful gardens. Gray Wolf waited, and watched, until the lovely princess came near to him, and then he sprang over the railings, seized her in his mouth, and ran away with her while her companions screamed in terror. On and on he ran, faster than the wind, until he reached the big oak tree where Ivan was waiting.

Now Gray Wolf called to Ivan, "Jump on! I shall carry you both."

So Prince Ivan and the Princess Helen sat on Gray Wolf's back as he raced toward the land of King Afron. At first the princess was very frightened, as well she might be, but Ivan held her, and calmed her, and before they reached Afron's kingdom the young couple had fallen in love.

"What am I to do?" cried Ivan, and wept as the moment to exchange the princess for the horse approached. If he did not hand over the lovely Helen to King Afron, his name would be dishonored and his father disgraced forever. And yet he could not give the princess up.

"Well," said Gray Wolf, "I have helped you this far, and I will help you one time more. Listen carefully: leave the princess here, and take me to the king instead. I shall change into the shape of the princess, and the king will not know the difference. He will give you the Horse with the Golden Mane, and you can ride away on it with the lovely Princess Helen."

Gray Wolf struck the earth with his paw, and in the twinkling of an eye changed into such a good likeness of the princess that no one could tell them apart. For once, Ivan did exactly as he was told, and was soon riding away on the back of the Horse with the Golden Mane. He and the princess had not ridden many days along the path before the wolf was suddenly there beside him again.

"How did you escape?" asked the astonished Ivan.

"For three days I lived in the palace, but I let the king see that I became more and more unhappy in such a prison, and on the fourth day I asked to take a walk outside. He loved me so much that he could not refuse me. Then, of course, I became myself again and ran away. Now let the princess ride the Horse with the Golden Mane, and you shall ride upon my back again, Prince Ivan. Quickly, for the king's guards are after us!"

But however fast the guards rode, Gray Wolf and the Horse with the Golden Mane ran faster, until at last the men gave up the chase. Soon the prince and his companions reached the land of King Dolmat, where the Firebird was to be Ivan's in exchange for the Horse with the Golden Mane. Ivan was deeply troubled. "How can I bear to leave this horse behind?" he moaned. "The finest horse I have ever seen, and now I have to give him up."

Gray Wolf sighed – if a wolf can sigh. Without saying anything, he struck the ground and turned into a likeness of the Horse with the Golden Mane. Ivan led Gray Wolf into the presence of the king, who was delighted with what he thought was the most magnificent steed in the world. He gave Ivan the Firebird, pardoned him for his theft, and let him go, having eyes only for the horse.

Prince Ivan took Princess Helen and the Firebird on the real Horse with the Golden Mane back toward his father's kingdom. They had not traveled far before Gray Wolf was by their side again.

"How did you escape this time?" asked the prince.

"I waited until the king rode me out on to the open plain," answered Gray Wolf, "and then I tossed him off my back and galloped away. Now I am myself again. And when we come to the place where I killed your horse, there I must leave you. I have served you well, and you can return to your own land with honor."

Prince Ivan was sad to see Gray Wolf go, but he had prizes beyond measure – Princess Helen, whom he loved dearly, the Horse with the Golden Mane, and the wondrous Firebird, of whom all had heard but few had seen. He was indeed a happy man.

Just before Ivan reached his father's palace, he stopped to rest from the fierce sun; the princess lay down under a tree, the horse was tethered in the shade, and the Firebird slumbered in her cage. Prince Ivan himself dropped into a deep sleep, and did not hear two men approach. They were his brothers, Dmitri and Vassily, who had returned empty-handed from their search and were now more bitter and resentful than ever when they saw that Ivan had won not only the Firebird, but a lovely princess and a fine horse as well. So they killed him. Dmitri took out his sword, chopped off Ivan's head, and cut up his body into little pieces. Then, pleased with their work, the two brothers grabbed the princess who awoke and screamed.

"You have killed my beloved! Oh, you cowards! How could you kill a man as he slept?" And she wept bitterly. The two brothers were not moved, however, and Dmitri pointed his sword toward her heart.

"You are ours now, Princess, and if you try to tell one word of what has happened, we will kill you too. The Firebird and the horse are ours too, and our father, the king, shall hear how we, not Ivan, have won them. Do you understand?"

The princess was terrified. What could she do but remain silent, although her heart was pierced as surely as if the eldest prince had plunged his sword into it. Then the two brothers drew lots for the prizes; Dmitri won the horse, and Vassily the princess. The Firebird was for their father, King Vyslav, since it was for this glorious bird that he had promised half of his kingdom while he lived, and the other half when he was dead.

The brothers rode back to the palace, where they were received with joyful celebrations. But all the while, Prince Ivan, who had risked everything, lay dead, his body scattered in the wilderness.

What more could occur, when death itself had claimed the prince? After thirty days, Gray Wolf came running through the same plain and he happened to see Ivan's body, and to recognize it. Just as he arrived, three ravens – a parent with two young ones – were about to start pecking at the remains. Swiftly, Gray Wolf took his chance, leaping upon one of the babies and seizing it in his jaws. The parent bird let out a terrible shriek. "Put down my baby, Gray Wolf! He has not done you any harm!"

"Only," said Gray Wolf, "if you will help me by going beyond the Thrice-Ten Kingdom and the Thrice-Nine Land to bring back the water of life and the water of death. Then I will release your child."

What could the parent raven do but agree? So he flew off, and in three days returned with the water of life and the water of death in two small flasks. Gray Wolf ripped the young bird apart. He sprinkled the water of death over it, and the bird was joined back together again. Then he sprinkled the water of life over it, and the bird flapped its wings and croaked a greeting to its parent. Now Gray Wolf turned to Ivan. He sprinkled his body with the water of death, and the wounds disappeared. Then he sprinkled his body with the water of life, and Ivan stood up. He rubbed his eyes, and said sleepily, "How long did I sleep for, Gray Wolf?"

"You would have slept forever," replied Gray Wolf, "if I had not saved you. But we have no time to lose. Your brothers have robbed you, and now Prince Vassily is about to marry Princess Helen the Fair. Climb on to my back, if you want to rescue her in time."

So Ivan and Gray Wolf sped away, faster than an arrow, faster than the wind, faster than lightning, and they arrived at the king's palace just as everyone was sitting down for the wedding feast. But when the princess saw Ivan, she leaped to her feet and called out, "This is my true husband! Now I am not afraid to speak!" And she denounced the two princes who had brought her there. King Vyslav was bewildered, for Dmitri and Vassily had told him that Ivan had died in the search, yet here was his beloved youngest son come back to life. When he heard the true story, his anger against his two eldest sons was so terrible that he ordered them to be thrown into a deep dungeon, and they were never heard of again.

So Prince Ivan reclaimed the Horse with the Golden Mane, and his lovely bride, Princess Helen the Fair. The king had the Firebird, and the young couple could celebrate their true marriage, and live in happiness for the rest of their lives.